AF425929

LOVE
DEATH and
NONSENSE

Also by John Wilson

<u>SELECTED NOVELS</u>

North with Franklin: The Lost Journals of James Fitzjames
The Journal of James Fitzjames: Facsimile Edition with
Illustrations
The Final Alchemy
The Heretic's Secret (single volume edition)
The Third Act
Written in Blood: The Complete Desert Legends Trilogy
The Ruined City
Lost Cause
Broken Arrow
Graves of Ice
Shot at Dawn
Lost Cause
The Alchemist's Dream
Wings of War: Tales of War book 1
Dark Terror: Tales of War book 2
A Dangerous Game: Tales of War book 3

<u>THE CAUGHT IN CONFLICT COLLECTION</u>

Four Steps to Death
Germania
Where Soldiers Lie
Lost in Spain
And in the Morning
Flames of the Tiger
Flags of War
Battle Scars
Death on the River

<u>SELECTED NON-FICTION</u>

Lands of Lost Content: A Memoir
A Soldier's Sketchbook: The Illustrated First World War Diary
of R.H Rabjohn
John Franklin: A Brief Biography
Norman Bethune: A Brief Biography

LOVE
DEATH and
NONSENSE

A diversity of verse.

John Wilson

Library and Archives Canada Cataloguing in Publication

Wilson, John (John Alexander), 1951 -
Love, Death and Nonsense/John Wilson

Many of these poems, or earlier versions of them, have been published over the years in *Amethyst Review*, *Canadian Author and Bookman*, *Quarter Moon Quarterly*, *Mainichi* and as part of *Lands of Lost Content: A Memoir*

Cover design and photography by John Wilson

Interior design and sketches by John Wilson

For more information on the author and his books, visit:

http://www.johnwilsonauthor.com

For Kevin Roberts, who told me at my very first public poetry reading that I had, "...wit, honesty and certainty."

Old Pictures

I am surrounded by the dead.
In sepia formality they hang
from the scaffold of the picture rail:
a great uncle killed at Loos
proud in his kilt
before the steamer's sad farewell;
his brother who survived
with a whole body
and forty years of a broken mind;
my grandmother
stern
Victorian
alone
in mourning black forever;
my parents' wedding
the groom alive with hope,
proud before an empire's collapse;
my mother at eighteen
between giggling sisters,
beautifully shy before the certainty of years.

All are gone,
only the bride's magnificent veil
lies, remembering
in an attic suitcase.

Yet still they live
within the walls of my imperfect memory,
and watch with timeless eyes
my life's amorphous dreams unfold.

Who will I look down upon
when I am clay and dust
and stoic, stand and stare
from far behind some dusty pane?

Last Call

"Last call for Flight 16."
To where?
My future,
hopeful, solid, imaginable,
a chaos of children,
journeys unforetold.
Your past?
Unfamiliar, ethereal, strange,
a different world
that I can never know.

"Will passengers proceed through Gate 3A."
I must go
while you recede through memories of
magic ships in deserts—port out starboard home,
bridge,
chota pegs beneath the waving punkah,
Mac, rabid enough to leave his teeth
imbedded in your gun,
great quakes of snaking rails, broken earth,
rescued infants in the Ayah's arms,
hailstones large as tennis balls,
tiger hunts and ponies gored by pigs unstuck,
and freedom, dohti-wrapped, that sent you home.
To what?
Sad memories of childhood loneliness
half spent in icy Fettes baths
before apprenticeships to rule,
hotels unvisited so long they must be but a dream,
shipyards dying of old-age,
used cars and ironmonger's shops,
and this and that,
until again the loneliness returns.

"Complete a customs form."
Declare my memories
of one who loomed so large he could do anything,
although that "damned bad hip" precluded any games.
Not true,
you taught me chess, whist,
to never blink at a royal flush,
to see the world as something magical,
how to fix a car,
to hold a silence which could sometimes scare me more than
any fist,
and how to live within myself,
you, who only really came alive
when conversations turned to thoughts of yesterday
across the world.

"I wish to hell I could come with you."
No.
There's just this one embrace,
the only one in forty years,
awkward, forgiving
a tear
no
look away
security is beckoning.

My father stands
a heavy shape
stick-propped
with only that damned cancer
for a friend.

Trains

Clickity-clack, clickity-clack.

Steam trains,
small mirrors with tiny gold letters
almost hidden in pretentious swirls.
Dark wood-glowing panels,
the smell of leather and always-full ashtrays,
the window's vertiginous drop
into the abyss between the seats,
revealing a perfect,
almost real, black-spotted world,
My mother,
swaying to the seductive motion of the carriage,
contemplating other trains, other lands,
other realities,
always with her back to the engine—
a life being dragged to the future
while regarding the past.
She kills her cigarette
and sighs,
unable to deny
the inevitable

clickity-clack, clickity-clack.

My Mother's Funeral

My mother loved to dance.
Through the glittering ballrooms of empire
she danced;
through the sirens and the flying bombs
she danced;
through my unforgiving childhood
she danced.

Now the damp grey air
has sucked the colour from the world.
Around a bottomless hole
we silently remember
the happy bright woman
who loved picnics in the woods
and the smell of babies
and try to ignore
the hopeless embarrassing sobs
of a weeping aunt.

Am I the only one
who wants to dance?

Skye

Where I grew up some folk believed
the calm intelligence of seals
in human guise could walk the land,
except on Sunday
when a God so stern
he would not let the ferries run held sway.
With *usquabae* the people talked
the ancient tongue of seers and poets;
so soft it made the wandering Danes remain
an age before the sound was turned to screams
beneath the redcoats' guns.

I remember fishing with my father
amongst the rocky barren isles,
wondering where the oily swell was from
while he read the waves
and told me of a dream he knew
where viceroys and beggars strode
across a scape of alien, shimmering beauty,
and sacred rivers washed the living and the dead.
A vanished world not happily exchanged
for this Atlantic cold.

In searching for that dream,
I ransacked Africa for gold and memories
and found dry hills and hatred;
I rummaged through the dusty wheaten prairie
where silent oceans lap the bones of dinosaurs
and found a rolling sky drowning in a
distant waterless horizon.

I travelled just to leave,
and found in frantic quest a circle of escape
ending nowhere.

It was all so long ago and near forgot,
but now I live again upon an island
perched upon the ocean's shuddering rim
and listen in the quiet lonely nights
for the seals to call me home.

My Father's Gun

My father's pistol lived in a metal box,
in the bottom of the wardrobe,
hidden from the children
beside the Christmas presents
in my favourite hiding place.

I loved that dark cave of musty smells and mothballs
on the borders of Narnia,
but mostly I loved the gun;
its weight that I could barely lift,
the blue-steel of its barrel,
the smell of its oil,
the roll of its name
Webley Scott.

With that gun I shot countless burglars,
and lions,
and bad guys,
and good guys,
and once, in an ecstasy of expectation,
we took it into a field and killed
a rotting tree stump.
For days afterwards my ears rang
and the bad guys exploded like dead wood.

Then one day the wardrobe contained
only lifeless clothes.
For an age I wondered if my father was a spy
who had to kill an enemy agent,
or if someone had stolen it
to return and murder us all.
How would I protect everyone
without my gun?

Eventually, I asked my mother,
"That old thing your father sold it
I never liked having it around."
So I went back to plastic guns,
but I knew I would
never again stand a chance
against the bad guys.

The Erskine Men

They must be gone by now,
the Erskine men of Christmas time
who came by childhood's door
to sell their home-made trinkets
from a wicker nest
too large to hold their dreams
yet far too small for even half their memories.

They always came in pairs,
these travellers in time
released from road-end buses
to walk in baggy coats that sagged
and let the chilling air blow through
just as it had along that icy Wipers trench.

Some hobbled on a leg of tin
or waved a sewn-up sleeve in flapping sad hello;
some stumbled blind
and caught a rough-shod foot upon
the ragged rims of shell holes long filled in;
some gasped for uncorrupted air
to fill the nearly useless lungs
that once could fill the Kop;
and some, on laughter-ridden streets
where we could only hear the cars,
abruptly huddled down
at noises much more ancient
remembering to always tilt
their helmets to the blast.

At school we made up stories of the ones who weren't let out
a harmless child's grotesquerie of gaping wounds still fresh
and hollow eyes and lipless screams
designed to scare
but in reality less horrible by far
than Erskine's hidden congeries of noble man's debris.

Some children, from the safety of their youthful vim,
would taunt these swaying distant men
with shrapnel sharp from lack of comprehension,
but older folk just watched
with silent looks I never understood
as their own sepia memories of missing loves and brothers
in poppy-red abandon staggered by.

They must be gone by now,
the Erskine men of Christmas time.
The long sad years of hopeless basket work at last undone.
I pray whatever black explosion
pushed them off our narrow ledge of sanity
was also strong enough to wipe away the hope
they never were to realize
before their world went mad.

The Erskine Hospital was a home for disabled soldiers near where I grew up. It
specialized in artificial limbs.
Wipers—soldiers slang for Ypres in Belgium.
the Kop—the Liverpool supporters end at Anfield football ground.

City Boy

I used to think myself a city boy,
a child of smoke-stained walls and traffic noise
and tenements of wailing kids and drunken dads.
I relished walking streets of unknown people
anonymous and grey.
I thrilled at older boys with
gang-badge-sharpened tail-combs
ready for a fight.
I knew the streets to run on feet spurred on
by flying diamond shards of bottle.
I knew the darkened bars where age was never asked
and scorned the threadbare nature of the local park
below the council flats with only its population of
strutting crows and begging ducks of lower class
where grass was only something
treacherous to hide the broken bottles.

But now my years of search have found another me.
A memory of ghostly, fertile fields where lived
Jemima Puddle Duck and friends.
Where, like as not when I awoke,
the kitchen table would be clothed
with corpses sad of still-warm rabbits,
helping to explain my dreams
of early morning firing squads.
A land of Gaelic mists
and ocean waves
which brought debris from other lands mysterious
which one day I would call my own.
pulled by the undertow of memory.

Which pole of truth should I pursue
as blindly stumbling on my road I go?
Who knows?

Glasgow Nights

Dark drunken Glasgow nights,
the sociability of bus stops
amidst the gobs of spit and wet discarded piles of
wasted beer and chips.
An old unshaven man prevents the stop from falling,
arms wrapped round the cold steel pole
with much more love than he has ever shown at home.
A pocket raggedly protects a brown-bagged bottle—
fortified, the label says,
as if its strength will stop the stomach heaves
and keep the drinker from the cold.

A boy goes past
nervously arrogant without his gang
caught halfway between being lord of the street
and just another one of father's punching bags.

A woman passes hurriedly, eyes down,
late shift at the hospital
already seen enough
to fill one night's imaginings.

Taxi's rumble by
distributing their loads
to other lives.

The old man coughs and swigs his wine
the bus is late—who cares
the stop is friendly,
what's to go home to anyway?
Kids have left,
silent wife'll never understand.
It's never been the same since shipyard closed.

He takes another drink, and slips
the bus stop, treacherous, has moved
betrayed a friend.
The bottle falls and breaks.
"Fuck," he slurs and weeps
to watch his hope run down the road.
Around his feet a blowing paper wraps
plastering his skinny legs.
An ineffectual kick opens up the sheet,
"Man Lands on Moon."
the headline reads.

Lunchtime Strip

The Friday lunchtime striptease crowd:
raucous denim
steel-tipped boots
trays of beer.
The dancer half-awake,
less exotic than the crowd,
gyrates to Aeorosmith
offering up herself
to feed the half-remembered fantasies
of half-a-hundred
marriage beds.

Young Jim is new at this
too shy to stare
he glances at the open nakedness
reflected in his glass,
and concentrates
on limp and tasteless fries.
His buddies banter at the girl
inviting her to join with them
in more ways than one.

The dollars offered
she collects
in any way her nakedness allows;
even Jim,
with sweaty palms and mumbled thanks,
manages to place his note upon the stage
rewarded with a smile of teasing promise
to bring the colour rushing to his cheeks.

A man alone,
middle-aged,
bespectacled,
Japanese.
His race sets him apart
much less than does
his pin-striped suit and tie
and offered twenty dollar bill.
She takes it,
anoints the queen with baby oil,

and listens as he talks
and points
and waves small scissors
and a folded card.
She shakes her head
moves away
forgetting to return
the money that she loved.

The show is done
the girl in open dressing gown
collects discarded clothes
each casual careless glimpse
of partly hidden flesh
now more erotic
than that freely offered
with the lunch.
"What'd he want?"
Jim's buddy asks.
"My pubic hair,"
she says,
"for his collection.
That's what's in the card.
He's been here every day this week.
Tips are getting bigger though,
if he gets to fifty
he can have some,
but I do the cutting."

She moves away
and Jim returns to work
to dream
not of her jutting breasts
and gleaming oily flesh,
but of a lonely man
whose intimacy
is catalogued by colour
in rows of private hair.

Home

A busy bridge.
Important people rushing home.
A crudely parked van.
A small noise.
A single shot.
"I thought it was a backfire"

I saw you fall
reflected in the paint of someone's shiny BMW
and took you home.
"Look what I found today."
You joined us for dinner,
a black presence
stifling conversation,
yet somehow belonging,
part of a family at last,
until the evening news
spread you too thin
and, fading,
you bade the world
you barely knew
farewell.

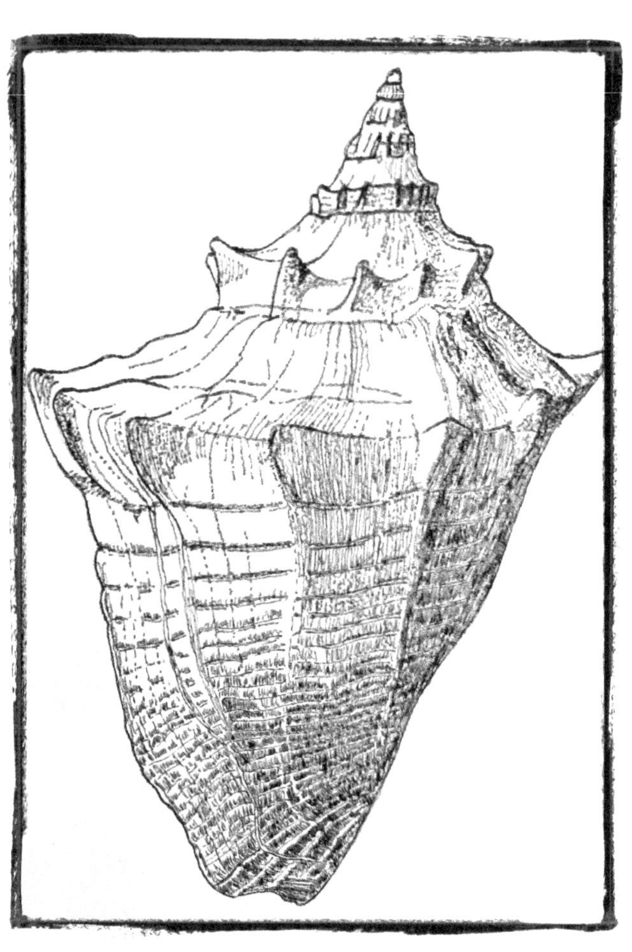

A Poem for   Two Voices

apartment 235

an aging refugee from

the simple country life

and one too many beatings

safe at last in a

quiet haven midst the traffic

I watch her from my window

battling along our back alley

against defiant dandelions

born of trash and engine oil

"the apartment's pretty
and
there are no stairs
and
neighbours are nice
and
my leg only hurts in the cold
and
there's the club twice a week
and
the park is close by
and
my balcony faces south
and
I have my window box
and
all say how well I've settled
but
I miss my garden so"

Yesterday's Weeds

Yesterday I saw her,
a bulbous body perched
upon the stick-like legs of age,
a once-dreamt Bosch monstrosity
symbolizing
futility.

My window frames her fight
with endless nature's chaos,
the faded scarf and beak-like nose searching
for offending propagators
of wilful green disorder.
Claw hands like bird's feet
striving for the brief breathless struggle
with recalcitrant roots,
each muddy victory marked
by spastic jerks of satisfaction.

At night in silent hells
of dandelions and crabgrass,
she longs for frost-patterned puddles
and crackling fallen leaves to signal
the deadly cold of winter's truce.
Awaking to the sun,
the ceaseless round continues
to ancient whispered curses
thrown at the carelessly fertile sky—
victualer of her enemies.

She hates me for my lazy yellow-spotted lawn
and I her for the compulsive absurdity
with which she distributes guilt
amongst us alley-dwellers.

Today the weeds riot,
soft fall breezes bid them bow
before the slowly passing limousine.
The battle is done,
I have lost,
my empty window weeps.

Hold My Hand

A maple-rich fall.
Come down with me,
through footstep-crunching leaves.
We'll watch the trains
and step outside,
the race already run.
What need of eyes to see the past?
What need of mouth to utter pain?
Or ears to hear a lie?
No womb-borne child
of mine will weigh
this planet down.

Hold my hand
my sad Pauline.
Your hair is messed
but who will see us now.
It's all been said and done,
except this one adventure,
black and new.

Come lie across the steel.
There are no heroes any more,
we'll wait in vain.
Feel the earth vibrate
pregnant with the coming night.
Hold my hand tight.
Don't cry,
scream with joy,
against the noise.

Indian Image 1—Goa

Awake to a room by the beach at Goa,
a high white cave of slumbering heat,
the lazy fan painting the walls
with brush-strokes of wave sound.

Outside the endless sands
preserve the naked footprints
of a thousand gods
sandwiched 'tween the layers of crashing waves,
and ghosts of fevered Jesuits,
gaunt as Greco Christs
and vying still for puny man's eternity,
haunt the tombs of mouldering laterite Notre Dames
to whisper in the souls of travellers,
while miracles still keep the flesh and bone of Xavier
as young as yesterday
before the wondering eyes
of faithful tourists.
He remembers once
long years ago
a woman overcome with ecstasy,
perhaps the one true convert,
bit a toe from off that sacred foot.

Awake again beneath bejeweled Ganesa
huge amidst his happy fragile acolytes
a garish ponderous rolling bulk
of comfort peace and succour
celebrating as he smiles enormously
the rotund joviality of our too brief lives.
If he were mine I would not give him up
to drink the blood and eat the flesh
of promises uncertain
and days of pain and thorns and suffering.

Indian Image 2—Kajuraho

High upon the dusty Deccan plateau
I sit amongst the dancing ancient stones
while prancing priapetic princes
copulate with energetic friends
and happy jewelled concubines
in mock disapprobation
avert their eyes and preen themselves
for pleasures ever to be locked in stone.

Did Kajuraho's princes fight and kill and die
as princes have been wont to do?
Were pleasures taken as reward for valour
or with captive fair or bestial?
If so they did not think it true enough
to be immortalized in stone
for here no one can die, except perhaps from ecstasy,
and days in endless leisure spent
pile one atop the next to reach
the sacred mountain peak.

This culture of unbridled joy
eight centuries before I came
could celebrate with such abandon
as to make the silent rocks alive
and tell this tale so unalike
the grubby world of now
where loveless gods look down
and sneer at our sad procreation.

Otzi

The cold eats through your bones,
the blinding snowflakes freeze your beard,
and leather straw and wool have lost their power to warm.
You stumble on on feet of lead
a roaring fire, a waiting wife
the only impetus for that next agonizing step.
A feather bed of snow beneath the wind,
you lay your quiver knife and axe aside and rest

Fifty centuries of calm blue ice muffle with equal ease
an army's thunderous tread and the whisper of a thought.
Asleep you lie
as Hannibal passed by fooled by Rome's eternity
and Christ fished in waters deeper than your sleep.
Your changeless dreams
a simple hut on legs beside a lake
a hearth
a meal of fish and grain
a family to pass your memory down.
Poor fool even the lake has long since gone.

The ice withdraws
and leaves you naked in our questing glare,
an ancient man so primitive
and yet so much like us.
We probe in awe
the arrow in your back,
the sacred marks upon your skin,
each tiny seed of gruel from your final meal,
and catalogue your trinkets tools and garb
as through those hollow eyes you watch our petty quarrelling

I want to touch your face
feel the skin's dark leatheriness
let you know I am alive
and care.
Maybe then you will awake
and forgive us for killing you.

For James Fitzjames

The final heartbeat runs
from deep within this shrunken form
huddled now beneath the curving oaken staves,
along the thread of pale and fragile warmth,
painted through this half-remembered land.

Like cat-discarded yarn it winds
between the piles of sculpted summer snow,
around deceitful floes which, having so betrayed our cause,
now break to open up a lead—a last ironic smile.

It snags upon the frost-bleached bones
exposed amidst the tattered scraps of blue
and swirling last requests unread,
'neath fallen tents where frozen fingers
clutch their pencils still.

It rigs, the skeletons of once-proud sunken ships
now crewed by memories
and haunted by the ghosts of hope.

It hesitates, by lonely cairns of stone
and by the lucky graves as yet unrobbed
of friends forever sketched,
like dancing insubstantial wraiths, upon the endless night.

In mounting fear of this sad place,
it races by the undiscovered points of land
whose names will never now be known,
past shattered cliffs of some time-frozen, tropic ocean,
out over raging waves and shimmering bergs,
to softer worlds of soot and grass and earth.

A four year length of twine
retraced in but a moment by this beat
ending where you stand,
shivering beside a roaring hearth
while, through the tears,
you gaze upon
the leaded crystal shards around your feet
and feebly try to haul me home
before the thread dissolves.

That
Old
Lie

Words of War

OUR wars are just.
WE are right.
GOD is on OUR side.
WE must win!

WE have reporting guidelines and press briefings.
THEY censor news and spout propaganda.

OUR bombs are environmentally sensitive.
THEIRS pollute indiscriminately.

OUR rockets are precise and humane.
THEIRS are random and poisonous.

OUR leaders are assured statesmen.
THEIRS are demented evil tyrants.

WE attack pre-emptively.
THEY launch sneak attacks without provocation.

OUR dead babies are innocent civilian casualties.
THEIRS are unavoidable collateral damage.

WE are professional, cautious, resolute, brave, desert rats.
THEY are brainwashed, cowardly, ruthless, fanatical, mad dogs.

WE take out eliminate, neutralize, attrit.
THEY destroy and
kill
kill
kill.

OUR wars are just.
WE are right.
EUPHEMISM is on OUR side.
THEY must lose!

Lebanon—10/23/83

The crispness of the morning air
took me on a fishing trip
to some lost Adirondack lake,
or Rocky Mountain trail,
or Arizona desert dawn.
To simple homes
a million miles beyond
this sad and ancient land.

Returning to a distant hum,
a speeding truck beneath the sun-touched roofs,
a singing dot,
where no foot touched a brake,
growing to fill my world.
Barrier, compound, front door blur
as eagerly the spinning wheels
make their obscene rendezvous.

What elder God smiles down
upon the righteous zeal
of this young martyr's fiery end?
What forces move his feet and animate his hands
to drive a half a ton of death
before my sleepy eyes?

This is his land,
its morning sun should call him
from a love amongst the cedars.
Life is brief enough beneath these weathered hills
for which crusaders yearned.
Why choose to end it all
in headlines dust and mourning?

I am the only one who saw his face
in those few final seconds
of a quarter thousand lives.
Was he filled with holy ecstasy
or warped by unimaginable rage?
I do not know.
I only know he looked at me
and smiled.

Lines on a photograph from the Holocaust

In moments uncluttered by life
your face returns across
the grainy, empty years:
your one escape,
an impossible flight
through the tiny timeless lens
which holds us both together
and apart.

On your arm,
a neatly folded overcoat,
the one you took on family walks
while noisy children teased your cautious fear
of unexpected showers
and coldly whispering winds.

But seasons end;
an awkward soldier stands behind,
too young to hold the clumsy rifle still,
and offers you the Earth
to be an overcoat.

Do you still stare at him,
across the pit
into the ageing nights he stole?
Does he awake and start
to see once more your head
swim in the gunsight of memory?

We are both lost,
the soldier and I,
within the tidy folds
and pointless sad humanity
of useless overcoats.

俳句

butterfly on a leaf
sips dew above
my father's grave

soaring sunlit cedars
small child stumbles
on a root

drifted blossom
filling carved letters
R.I.P.

prairie backroad
slow funeral procession
past dinosaur bones

spring rain
drips in the hearts of
tomorrow's mountain

crushed parchment leaf
on an asphalt driveway
a child's first step

holly berries
Christmas spots of blood
on my finger

bookends in the park
two vets. share a bench
one leg each

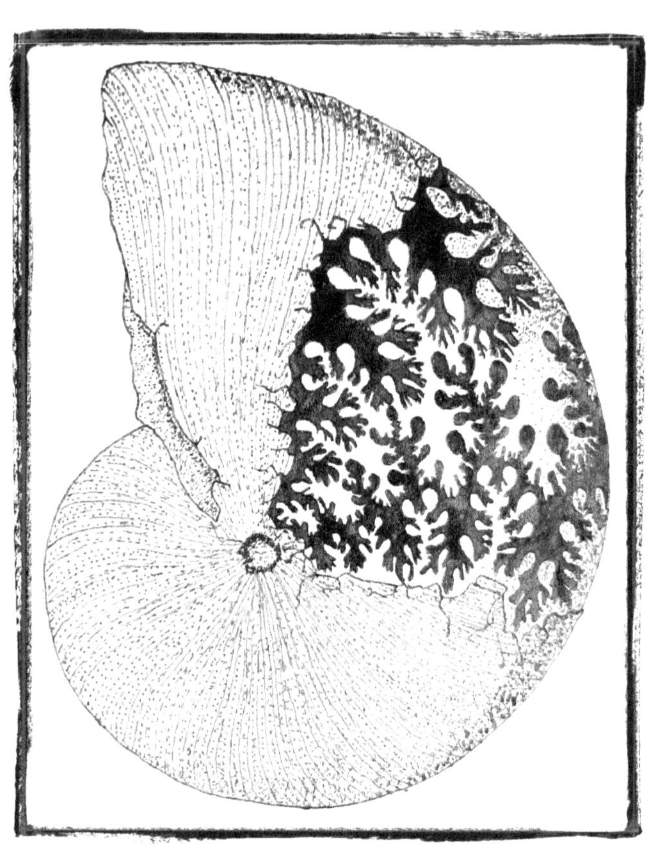

Peach Tree

Outside my window
you stand deceptively frail,
on the edge of your known world,
each year struggling
to thrust a few small hopeful fruit
into terra incognita
while dreaming of California.
Beside you a fir grows,
robust, solid, Canadian.
It knows mountains
and thrives on winter's chill,
yet it does not mock
your sad transplanted bravery.
With open pine-clothed arms
it welcomes your variety,
but, like me,
your immigrant's heart
can never be truly
at home beside it.

After You've Gone

You were not here
to greet the tide
when it came sidling up
to lap around our door,
and so it left
in slow sorrow down the shingle.

The moon arose in solemn pomp
to pass the nighttime hours
in talk of cheese and lunacy,
you were not here
and so it left
upon its long decaying arc.

The continents no longer slide
upon the ocean plates
and glaciers cry milky tears
and sit upon the mountaintops
to wrap themselves in foggy loneliness.

This morning my kettle made two cups of tea
to sit in accusatory silence
upon the desolation of my countertop,
you were not here
and so I drank them both.

Now I shall go down and sit
beside the crying waves
and see if the tide bothers to return.

An Insanity of Gardening

The bees have drained the flowers.
Nectar-drunk they realize that flying is impossible
and crawl beneath cold stones
to hug their furry abdomens,
and fondly recollect a happy dance
on honey-laden hives.

Earthworms conquer flight.
On tiny wings of gossamer they carry vital mail
between nasturtium continents
while gazing down on beetles,
ironclad and rumbling
with blitzkrieg speed
to breach the lines of worried ants
and thrust towards
some distant, grassy Stalingrad.

Beside the herbs the butterflies
are bombing helpless lines of ladybugs
who push their prams of mattresses
towards their fiery homes.

From my imposing perch,
I sit and watch while uncontrolled
my hand with spastic jerks destroys
the little scrap of paper
in which you say farewell
and turn my garden mad.

Love Song

If I were not Alexander
I would be Diogenes.
Would you love a dog as much,
sitting in a clay tub
ignoring mad thoughts of conquest?

If I were Diogenes
I would not be Alexander,
and Darius would sleep easy in Persepolis
while you could stand between the sun and I
to cloud these cynic thoughts.

But I am me,
a featherless cock,
hopeful lantern clutched
to seek an honesty
bright enough to dull Athenian suns.
Do not laugh.
If I were not Diogenes
I would be me–
and still love you.

Communion

One hundred billion
and one.

Wolf it down,
it's your duty.

A hurried communion of greasy souls.

Dip the fries in ketchup.
Suck their torn and bleeding necks.

Raise the cup.
This is my blood you drink.

In the kitchen the loaves and fishes—
eternally dividing.

It is done.

I have to leave
and in the parking lot,
write a poem.

A Similarity of Nuns

There is a similarity
to nuns of later years,
the short-cut, greyish hair
well-groomed but sensible,
the cream, loose-fitting blouse
and patterned skirt above
the leather sandals which have trod God's path so long.

The faces too are similar,
two eyes with patience in their depths
and lips perpetually in smile
at some great cosmic joke
all set within a rugged skin
sun-wrinkled from long years in Africa or Ecuador.

It is, I would suppose,
a similarity of purpose
that creates such visages,
just as the owner of a dog becomes
with time more mongrelish.
I wonder if, behind those looks
of reassuring calm, they miss
the variegated sins
of our less contemplative lives.

Dying

I do not want to die
between two cold and antiseptic sheets
while nurses tend
the hum and beep of some machine
which tells them when the bed is free.
I do not want my body
to be washed and scrubbed and
made presentable
for relatives who'll say
"It's for the best he's gone."

I want to go and sit beneath a tree
and feel the earth between my toes.
I want to breathe in gulps of air unpurified,
and chew the stems of unhygienic grass
while ants begin to plan my journey home.
I want to die with dirty fingernails.

Dinosaur Tooth

seventy

five

million

years

of sleep

waiting

for this day's sun

and my transient touch

your fearsome edge no longer

tears through flesh past bones

now turned to stone

puny I will never run in fear

from your remembered victories

slavering and bloody

instead I'll sit you on my desk

a harmless curio for idle chatter

never suspecting your wish

to tear out my throat

for disturbing

seventy

five

million

years

of sleep.

My Office

In orange shorts and carpet slippers
surrounded by the books of others
I sit alone beneath the family noise
and write.

The flickering screen alive with
fine imaginings
or dead with turgid images
and cliched coprolites.

The keyboard's busy clack
or the silence of sleep
are mine alone to know
in the long hours between the
postman's hopeful step.

Thoughts pregnant with
the power to change the course of continents
or too weak to stagger off my fingers,
both will stay and echo round the walls
of this benighted room
long after I have gone to join
the simple happy noise of children.

Poetic Dreams

I want to be a poet
You know what I mean
I want to get the words to rhyme
And scan without a seam
I want to tell your highest thoughts
Surprised by fine excess
If truth be beauty, beauty's truth
I must not strive for less

But feet and ictus leave me cold
As does a compound trochee
Acatalectic verse what's more
Could be my Aunty Strophe

For when I sit to scan my ream
My messy mind begins to dream
Of photogenic serpentine
And Mr Clean's new prayer machine
And gasoline in the Pleistocene
And aubergine from Aberdeen

So I reflect as I sit back
To let the metre flow
The road of Keats is hard to take
It's steep and sharp and slow
Perhaps I should just stick to prose
That is much better paid
And tell myself that poets true
Are all in heaven made.

Old Friend

Today I slew a trusty friend
Of twenty-seven years
He'd stuck by me through thick and thin
And shared my doubts and fears.

The sixties saw us wild and free,
The seventies were dull.
In eighty-two I bought a suit,
Employers for to lull.

We had good times despite all that,
You shared my soup and beer.
We kissed the selfsame pretty girls
And married the same year.

The nineties loom before us now
And we are both quite grey.
I realize that I have hid
Behind you every day.

And so you see I had no choice
It is the day you feared
This morning I awoke resolved
And shaved off all my beard.

The Streets of Nanaimo

They stride toward me faces gleaming
Muscles pumping, sweat glands streaming.
No Macedonian phalanx strong
Scared Darius more in days long gone
Than this designer headband wearing
Pastel blur of healthy bearing.
They look at neither sky nor sea,
But straight ahead at cringing me.
At last I break and in the broom
I hide as down the path they loom
And pray that God will save me please
From energetic retirees.

A Farewell to Alberta Friends

We have to say goodbye to you
From Georgia's soggy strait
You're returning to the prairies now
Before it gets too late

But just in case your memory
Has mildewed in the rain
Here's one or two reminders
Which just might save you pain

First dig out your cowboy hat
And boots and spurs and tackle
Then learn to spell Dwight Yoakum
That's really half the battle

De-rust the trusty snow shovel
You know the drifts are coming
And never, never, ever laugh
At Willie Nelson's strumming

Immerse yourselves in culture pure
And learn the local slang
For lunch you catch some growlies
And cuss at k. d. lang

Buy two rusted pickup trucks
To find them is not hard
Onc should run, the other's just
To decorate the yard

When going to the local inn
Drink rye and beer, no more
And only buy sweet sherry at
A distant liquor store

But seriously we'll miss you more
Than poetry can say
But that won't stop us laughing
From November through to May

And if by chance some oil they find
Outside your own backdoor
Then don't forget your moss-hung friends
By Lantzville's pebbly shore.

Hard Times

Evangelist on television
Praying for my soul
It seems his God is short of cash
And needs a new bankroll

He never did get paid, I guess
For six long days of toil
And ever since He's worked so hard
His creditors to foil

The Bank of Heaven's at the gate
Demanding harsher measures
A balanced budget, zero debt
And sale of family treasures

So valiant Micheal's been let go
His sword and armour dusty
And poor old Peter's on half time
And lets the gate get rusty

Fifty angels were laid off
Poor things they had no say
Even Satan felt the pinch
And roasts just once a day

I'd like to help, I really would
But what I do is write
And from a fiscal point of view
That is a sorry plight

We're short of cash, this God and I
From heavenly recession
But thinking hard on God and Man
I have a small suggestion

If God can make the grass to grow
Then surely He can stop it
And I could sell my lawnmower
And we could share the profit

Likewise food can eat up cash
From prime steak to banana
Now I could save a bundle with
A freezer full of manna

And if my hot tap gave me wine
My cold one could give beer
And God and I could pay our debts
And soon be in the clear

It is a brilliant thought, I think
And bound to make a splash
There's just one thing that bothers me
Where would I send the cash

Travelling without leaving home

Oh Martha look, the Taj Mahal
see how it glitters so
a masterpiece of ancient art
oh damn, its time to go

Oh Martha see, a Raphael
its filled with life and hope
the form, the lines remind me so
of that old ad for soap

Oh Martha hear, the symphony
the crystal, dulcet tones
its good to sit in here awhile
and rest the tourist's bones

Oh Martha now, how meaningful
affirmative not bitter
those zen boys really knew the way
to rake out kitty litter

Oh Martha well, at last were home
to Kansas we're returning
with souvenirs and photographs
and not one ounce of learning

Dinosaur BBQ

Now once upon a long long time when all was clean and new
The mammals got together to host a barbecue

They asked the mighty dinosaurs who ruled that far off land
If they would kindly join them in their feast upon the strand

The dinosaurs arrived in style for lunch on New Year's Day
Led by tall tyrannosaurus in waistcoats made of grey

He brought apatosaurus, much bigger than a house,
And baby ceratopsians, no larger than a mouse.

Down walked parasaurolophus, pteranodon (who flew)
Stegosaurus, triceratops and plesiosaurus too.

The food was all laid out upon great tables on the sands
The lemonade and orange juice filled forty-seven pans.

While herbivores munched salad, the carnivores ate meat
And omnivores ate everything with cream to make it sweet.

They stuffed themselves with chocolate cake, spaghetti and
ice cream
Then all lay down and went to sleep and some began to
dream.

And as they dreamed the tide came in to join them in their
fun
But then it saw the food was gone, they'd saved it not a
crumb.

The tide got cross and stamped its foot, and swept them out
to sea
And that's why none are left today to frighten you and me.

Light and Dark

There's a sunrise every morning,
A sunset every night,
Between then both it's either dark
Or very, very light.

The Beglup shuns the light of day,
The Scribbling fears the dark,
Thus they will never ever meet
At dusk down by the park.

It cannot be both light and dark,
Tis either one or t'other.
So the Beglup and the Scribbling
Knew nothing of the other.

Until one eve the bright daylight
Was slow in going to bed
And darkness fell a bit too fast,
Or so it has been said.

In any case, for one bright blink
In darkness thick as leather,
The Scribbling fierce and Beglup bold
Were face-to-face together.

They stopped and stared, then screamed and fled,
Their meeting could not be
For each was far too frightful for
The other one to see.

The Aardvark's Supper

So darkly, darkly shines the moon
At night on Christmas Day
When down below in silver hue
The three-legged fishes play.

They leap and jump o'er hill and dale
So happy to be free
From that sticky pea-green ocean
Which hides them all from me.

They sing a sort of fishy song
In scales of their own choice
Without a single thought or care
For danger's lovely voice.

From out the east the Aardvark comes
With jaws as wide as stairs
To feed upon the happy fish
Who frolic unawares.

"Oh comely, comely little fish,"
The earth-pig sings out loud,
"Jump on my glittering spoon
And we shall dine most proud."

The fishes wander to-and-fro
Enraptured by the tune
And one by one they step upon
The Aardvark's dining spoon.

When sudden one small voice is raised
Amidst the wails and tears,
"I cannot hear enticing tunes
There's darkness in my ears."

Then quickly quickly little fish
Pluck darkness from the night
And stuff it in your tiny ears
To quell the sound and fright.

The Aardvark blusters "Come back here!"
As fishes skip away
Back to the hilly sea they run
To swim another day.

The Aardvark glumly then goes home
With rumbling, empty tummy
To dine on porridge and brown toast
And cups of dark red honey.

We came upon a funny thing

We came upon a funny thing
no bigger than a mouse.
Its coat was blue, its eyes were green,
it ran about the house.
For you are only three times two
and everything is all so new.

"Oh look," I said, "it's snuffling
and running to and fro."
"Oh no," you said, "that isn't true,
it's sniggling oh so low."

"It's not," I said, quite vigorously,
prepared to rave and rant.
"Snuffling noise I know about,
which at your age you can't."

"But Dad its nose so long and thin,
it twists so grumphily
That snuffling is impossible,
it's plain as plain can be.

"It sniggles as it goes around
and sheds a silver tear
Put aged ears down close by it
and you will surely hear."

I listened then with bated breath
to noises soft and slow
And then at last I heard the beast
was sniggling oh so low.

Apologies for doubting
what you ever said was true
You see the world much clearer now
than I can ever do
For I am only forty-two
and everything is all so new.

The Seven Deadly Sins

For writers as for normal folk
The seven sins are not a joke
But I am doomed before I start
For sin is such a part of art
On lust and wrath my stories thrive
And greedy dreams of wealth my drive
My sloth is passed off as reflection
But pride I need to salve rejection
I glut myself on words of gold
And envy stories better told

Lust
I love you more than I can say
And think about you night and day
My waking hours your image fills
And you my dreaming body thrills
You are my life, my hope, my breath
And I shall love you unto death
No other love will I allow
For none can match our holy vow
When once a year I bare my breast
And send my writer's grant request

Wrath
Oh slavering, mewling, gutless swine
Spewing wisdom thought divine
You dare reject yet cannot do
The priceless work I send to you
You do not know the field I plow
My thoughts go sailing past your brow
And yet you say, you witless peasant
"We cannot use your work at present."
I hope the devil too abhors
The hellish host of editors

Avarice
I want a place where I can write
Beside the ocean calm and bright
From three miles down my private drive
I'll watch the eagles soar and dive
And on my desk of solid gold
I'll write great works already sold
But ere I reach these vulgar heights
There's just one thing to put to rights
The payment for my poems has been
Two copies of the magazine

Sloth
In Wordsworth's quiet reflective dream
I sit and watch the tidal stream
Without the busy keyboard's clack
Of time I fear I have lost track
I tell myself that this is work
We poet's need this nature's perk
To clear the mind of life's mundane
And trivial little daily strain
But if you wish the truth be told
I'm half asleep and too damned cold

Pride
When I write my next great work
No longer in the shade I'll lurk
Awards will shower upon my head
With Mr. Booker I'll to bed
My bank account will swell and grow
And I shall host a late night show
A household name I will become
As I shall strike the critics dumb
But 'fore the spark of fame doth glint
I'll have to get my work in print

Gluttony
Give me a line, a phrase, a word
It matters not that it's absurd
I'll take them all and then some more
And stuff myself from Oxford's store
On oxymorons I will feast
With verbs and nouns I'll be a beast
I'll read and read and read and read
Until my eyes begin to bleed
And when I'm full and nothing's new
I'll say it all in one Haiku

Envy
My dog lies sleeping in my room
Untroubled by my scribblers' gloom
She doesn't care she cannot talk
Her words are only food and walk
Her brain seeks not philosophy
But dreams of bones and strolls with me
Right now her role is hard to top
My pen for fleas I'd gladly swap
And I could sleep upon a whim
And she could write this bloody poem

So when the judgement day draws nigh
And it is time to say goodbye
I shall not hope I'm bound for heaven
Remembering just the deadly seven
And comfort I shall draw in part
If I am quick and very smart
The competition's fierce I know
I'll shine my prose before I go
And luck might land me at the bell
A column in The Daily Hell.